# THE THANKABLES®

## Three Little Creatures With Very Large Features

## STORY BY NAYOMI THOMAS
### ART BY RACHEL KORHONEN

Books may be ordered through Amazon.com or by contacting:

P.O. Box 18 Grandview, MO 64030
phone: 402.855.4673
email: thethankables@gmail.com
**www.thethankables.com**
facebook.com/thethankables
twitter.com/thethankables
instagram.com/thethankables

Because of the dynamic nature of the Internet, any web addresses or links contained in
this book may have changed since publication and may no longer be valid.

ISBN-13:978-1539059462
ISBN-10:1539059464

Library of Congress Control Number: 2013915114
Printed in the United States of America.

Art By Rachel Korhonen

Design and Layout By:
Phillip Ortiz
Peel Creative LLC
www.peel-creative.com

To my daughter Mahan Gabriela Thomas, whose smile reminds me daily to be thankful!

In everything give thanks; for this is God's will for you in Christ Jesus. 1 Thess. 5:18

It was a certain afternoon and not a thing seemed right.
Our car was broke and money spent; there was no hope in sight.
Around my house the scene was gloomy and joy did not shine.
Mom and Dad were on the couch. I could see they were not fine.
My older brother Jude and I sat restless on the floor.
When suddenly, with a BIG BOOM! flew open the front door.

And standing there in our house were three strange little creatures.
The first things I saw were their very gigantic features.
They had great big, beautiful, sparkling eyes round as a ball,
And such GINORMOUS floppy ears that helped them hear it all.

We stared in shock, as they walked to the center of the room.
As they drew close we heard them hum a happy HOPE-filled tune.
With the first beat they boogied and their hips began to swing.
They opened their mouths wide and big and then began to sing.

I grinned at my brother and shouted, "What a funny song!"
And POOF, as quickly as they came, in a flash they were gone.
"Wait! wait!" I stood up and spun, "Did they have to leave so fast?!"
Mom and Dad giggled and jumped, saying "My what a blast!"
Mom held us by the hand and said "These creatures they are right.
The things that made our family sad had not been worth the fight."
We realized that our gloom had not been good. Not at all.
Instead we should be thankful, in the big and in the small.

I was certain that forever our worries were gone.
Sad to say, that the next day, troubles came back with the dawn.
My parents, they were arguing. I know I heard them shout.
Their hearts began to fill again with gray and gloomy doubt.

They were talking about dollars and not having enough cents.
Bills were due, the roof leaked they sounded very tense.
I did not like to hear Mom and Dad so very mad.
It made my brother Jude and I feel gloomy and so sad.

When suddenly, like lightning, the front door burst open, WHACK!
Those peculiar creatures had just suddenly come back!
This time those big brown eyes looked at us kindly but sincere.
They didn't like that we listened to the spirit of fear.

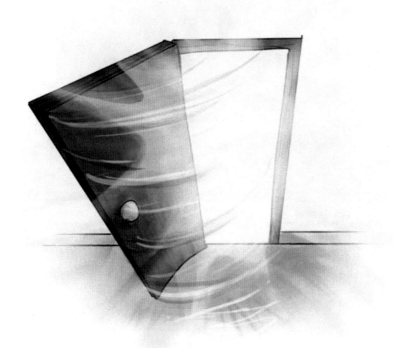

They sang much, MUCH, MUCH louder than they had the time before.
It almost matched the volume of our Grandpa's loudest snore!
They stood there in the center of our humble living room,
To remind us God is good through that joyful little tune:

Once again POOF, like the first time, the three creatures were gone!
We were gently humbled hearing again their hope-filled song.
This time I was pretty sure, we all knew where they were from,
And Who had sent them just for us, and even why they'd come.
We laughed and laughed all through the day and all the way to bed.
This time we would not forget to always be thankful instead.

That night I realized that those creatures had been a gift.
So I prayed for all my friends whose spirits needed a lift.
Some of them live in a city without a big blue sky.
They may not have a grandma who bakes them a yummy pie.
And perhaps at night they cannot sleep and lie wide awake.
Some of them are hungry or maybe have a tummy ache.

Dear Jesus help us hear you and listen to you close.
There's always hope in you, Yes! You love us the most!
You're the Son of God, who carried the cross to Calvary.
You gladly gave your life for us you died to set us free.
Help us trust in you; simply believe that your words are true.
Give us RIGHTEOUSNESS, HOPE and JOY when we say yes to you.
Jesus, please reveal yourself to us; reminding us you're near.
We'll be filled with a HOPE in God instead of earthly fear.
So when we feel that life is hard and the day is too long,
Help us remember this story and sing the creatures' song:

"Ohhhhhhhh thank you for the big blue sky
Thank you for Grandma's apple pie
Thank you Jesus you died for me
Now forever, Yay! I am free!

I have nothing I need to fear
Jesus you are always near
Good or bad we count it all joy
Aaaand in everything we give thanks!"

# The End

# 40 days
## #warongrumbling

**With the help of an adult write down each day what you are thankful for:**

*Hints, Truths about God, Your Family, Your Friends, Teachers, Health*

_____    _____

_____    _____

_____    _____

_____    _____

_____    _____

_____    _____

_____    _____

_____    _____

_____    _____

_____    _____

_____    _____

_____    _____

_____    _____

_____    _____

_____    _____

_____    _____

_____    _____

_____    _____

# THE THANKABLES®
## Songs!

are available for download at:

# www.thethankables.com

— *Also Available!* —

## THE THANKABLES®
## Children's Book Series

### "Do Not Worry, Do Not Fret"

Tilly, Lilly and Mom encounter various trials throughout their day. In each one, they are faced with fear. But the heavenly hosts with harmonies remind them of their power to chose gratitude so they can overcome.

Available at:
www.thethankables.com
or amazon.com

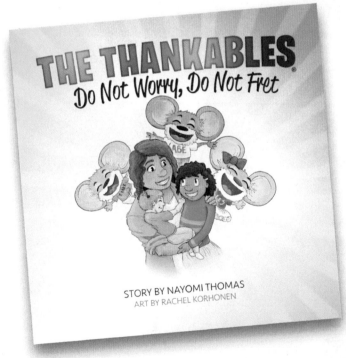

THE THANKABLES®
Do Not Worry, Do Not Fret

STORY BY NAYOMI THOMAS
ART BY RACHEL KORHONEN

Made in the USA
Columbia, SC
09 November 2021

48604251R00015